NOEL

An Unforgettable Night!

Preface

Dear friends, young and old,

I am about to tell you the beautiful story of the birth of Jesus. This happened a long, long time ago in Bethlehem in Judea.

Since Jesus came to earth for all people, in all places, I chose, for this story, to have him born in a place other than Palestine. I could have chosen Asia, or Africa, but I picked the Great North of Canada, which is so different from the mountains and deserts of Judea.

Of course, I kept the essence of the story, but added some different cultural elements to emphasize that God's love knows no bounds and no borders. Jesus came to tell the whole world that his Father's love is for all children on earth—whether from the Americas, Asia, Africa, Europe, or Oceania.

Now read and enjoy this wonderful story of Christmas.

Claire

Brief explanation of unfamiliar words

Nanuq White Bear
Ishumataq Wise hunter who provides food for others
Allaniq North
Quilliq Lamp or small stove made of soapstone. The soapstone is sculpted into a round form with a little basin on top to hold fuel. The *quilliq* burns with seal blubber.
Kometic Sled drawn by dogs and used by the Inuit
Nunavut Name of a geographic territory in the Canadian Arctic

NOEL

An Unforgettable Night!

Claire Dumont

ILLUSTRATED BY

Mehrafarin Keshavarz

Paulist Press
New York / Mahwah, NJ

My name is Mary.
I am the wife of Joseph.
We are expecting a baby.
We'll call him Jesus.

I am Joseph, Mary's husband.
I hunt and fish for food.
I live in *Nanuq*, a village in the Great North of Canada.

One day, returning from fishing, Joseph says,

"Mary! I learned that the great *Ishumataq* wants to know how many people live in the Great North of Canada. I'll have to register in *Allaniq*, the village of my ancestors."

"But Joseph, you know that I must go to my grandmother's home to give birth. The baby will be born soon."

"Mary, we are obliged to go."

"That's true, Joseph. I am worrying for nothing."

Mary thinks: we must bring blankets, a *qulliq*, oil… oh my goodness!

We must have clothing for the baby!

You never know…

A few days later, Joseph and Mary leave *Nanuq*.
On the road, they meet other travelers.
Some animals are curious and stop along the way.

Worn out and exhausted after days of travel, they finally arrive at the village of *Allaniq*.

Upon entering the village, Mary is surprised.
"Joseph, there will never be room for us here!"
"You're right. It's too late to register anywhere.
First we must look for a place to spend the night."

Joseph goes from one tent to the next.
There is no place for them.
Suddenly, he has an idea. He rejoins Mary.

"Mary, I remember that there was an ice cave not very far from here. What if we went there?

It will not be warm, but we will be sheltered and safe.

Are you able to continue?"

"Yes, Joseph. The baby is moving and I'm hungry."

As they leave the camp, they see the animals still following their *kometic*. Joseph presses on and finds the shelter.

"Come, Mary. The cave is empty. I am happy. We will be safe for the night."

"This is good, Joseph! We'll be fine here."

Quickly Joseph places
animal skins on the floor.
He worries about Mary.
What if the baby comes?
"Sit down, Mary. I am bringing
the *quilliq*. We will eat and rest."
"I'm not hungry anymore.
Instead I feel tired."
"Okay, I will bring in the dogs.
They will keep us warm."

Joseph leaves the cave:
"Oooh, how beautiful! The sky is full of northern lights!"
Suddenly, there is a cry:
"Joseph, Joseph! The baby, the baby is coming!"

That night, Jesus was born.
Mary wrapped him in cloths and then in furs.

Not very far away, on the ice, fishermen collect their catch. They say to each other:

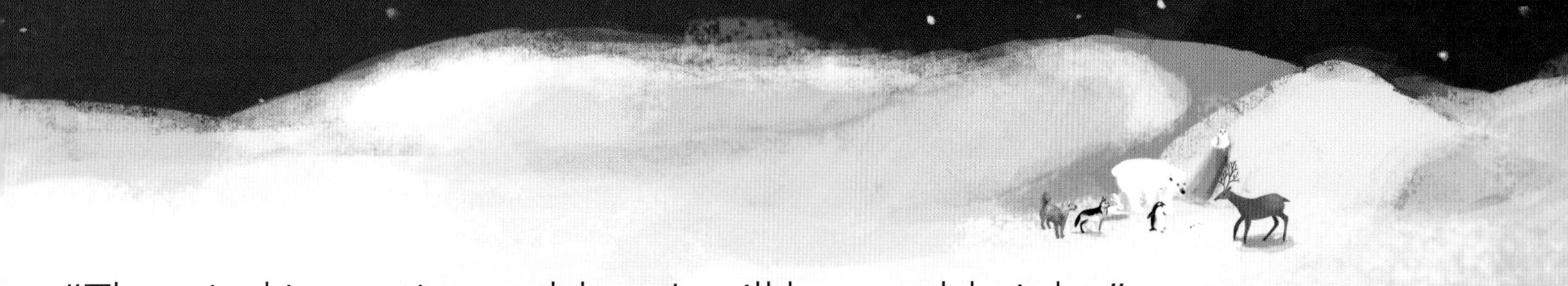

"The wind is starting to blow. It will be a cold night."
"Yes, but it is so beautiful. The sky is clear."

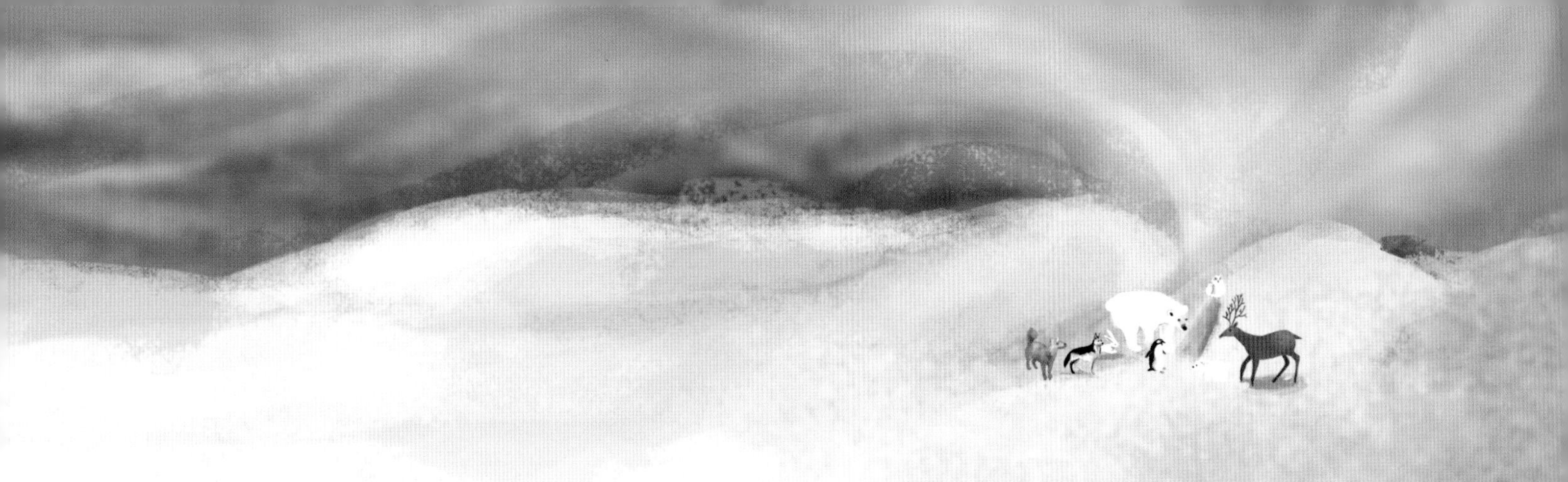

Suddenly, a light appears in the sky in the middle of the night.
They hear sweet sounds in the background.
It's strange. Surprised and scared, they wonder:
"What's happening?"
"Is that music?"
"No! I hear a voice."
"Listen! Listen!"

The music is lovely. The fishermen listen and hear:

"Do not be afraid! Today I give you great joy.

A child is born to you. Go to the cave. You will find a baby wrapped in furs. Praise be to him. Peace to all people on earth!"

And all of a sudden, nothing!
The fishermen are wondering if they dreamed it. They are silent for a long time.
Then they all start talking.

After much discussion, they decide to find out for sure what is going on and search for the cave together.

The quickest one, a young fisherman, cries out, "Come, come! I see a light in the cave!"

The curious fishermen eagerly approach the light.

They see a dad and a mom with a tiny baby.

Mary and Joseph are proud and happy to show their son to them: Jesus.

Enveloped by the magic of this sweet moment, the fishermen decide to spend the night with the small family.

It was the first Christmas.

An unforgettable night.

From their distant lands, three great *Ishumataqs* have already heard that a king would be born in the region of *Nunavut*.

Guided by a star, they arrive at *Allaniq*.

They pay tribute to Jesus and offer him beautiful gifts: gold, ivory, and furs. Although they do not know it, the *Ishumataqs* have met the King of kings.

Each year for more than two thousand years, all people who know and love Jesus gather on December 25 to celebrate Christmas.

Christmas is the birthday of Jesus, the King of the universe.

Christmas is when God comes to speak with the children, women, and men of all countries. Having become human, Jesus announces that God is a dad who loves all people on earth. He also says that happiness is loving one another.

Christmas is the great feast of LOVE, SHARING, and JOY!

Cover illustration by Mehrafarin Keshavarz

Originally published as *Noël: Une Nuit Inoubliable!* © 2015 by Éditions Médiaspaul
English translation copyright © 2017 by Paulist Press. Translated by Gloria Capik.

Library of Congress Cataloging-in-Publication Data

Names: Dumont, C. (Claire), 1950– author. | Keshavarz, Mehrafarin, illustrator.
Title: Noel, an unforgettable night! / Claire Dumont ; illustrated by Mehrafarin Keshavarz.
Other titles: Noël, une nuit inoubliable English
Description: New York : Paulist Press, 2017. | Summary: "Reimagines the familiar story of Jesus' birth as if it occurred in the snowy Canadian Arctic, among the Inuit people"—Provided by publisher.
Identifiers: LCCN 2017017680 (print) | LCCN 2017023947 (ebook) | ISBN 9781587687389 (ebook) | ISBN 9780809167807 (hardcover : alk. paper)
Subjects: LCSH: Jesus Christ—Nativity—Juvenile fiction. | CYAC: Jesus Christ—Nativity—Fiction. | Christmas—Fiction. | Inuit—Fiction. | Eskimos—Fiction. | Nunavut—Fiction. | Canada—History—Fiction.
Classification: LCC PZ7.1.D835 (ebook) | LCC PZ7.1.D835 No 2017 (print) | DDC [E]—dc23
LC record available at https://lccn.loc.gov/2017017680

ISBN 978-0-8091-6780-7 (hardcover)
ISBN 978-1-58768-738-9 (e-book)

Published by Paulist Press
997 Macarthur Boulevard
Mahwah, New Jersey 07430

www.paulistpress.com

Printed and bound in the United States of America
By Versa Press, Peoria, Illinois
August 2017